AMORAK

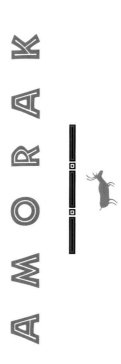

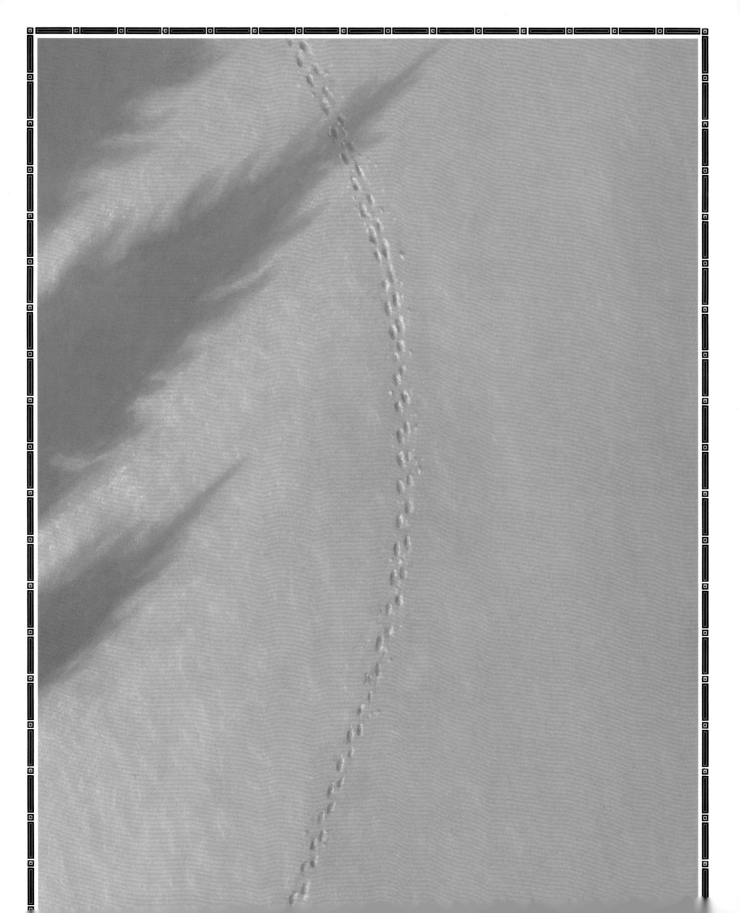

A·M·O·R·A·K

Story and Illustrations by Tim Jessell

CREATIVE EDITIONS

For Ragan, Mom, and Dad.

Designed by Jane Palecek
Art Director: Rita Marshall

First published in 1994 by Creative Editions
123 South Broad Street
Mankato, Minnesota 56001

Creative Editions is an imprint of The Creative Company.
This title is published as a joint venture between The Creative
Company and American Education Publishing.

Library of Congress Cataloging-in-Publication Data

Jessell, Tim.

Amorak / Tim Jessell.

Summary: In this retelling of an Inuit creation myth, Grandfather
explains why the caribou and the wolf are brothers.

ISBN 1-56846-092-9

1. Inuit – Legends.   2. Tales – Alaska.   3. Tales – Canada.
[1. Eskimos – Legends.   2. Indians of North America – Legends.
3. Caribou – Folklore.   4. Wolves – Folklore.] 1. Title.

E99.E7 J58   1994
398.2′089′971 – dc20
[E]   93-48622   CIP   AC

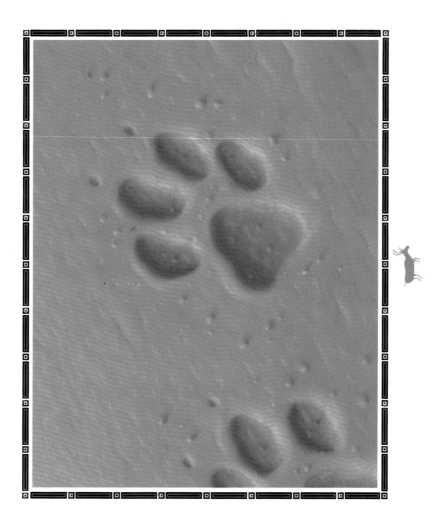

A howl split the air as my grandfather tucked me into bed. "Don't be afraid," Grandfather said, "the caribou and the wolf are brothers." I shook my head. "Brothers don't eat each other. I've seen the wolf hunt the caribou many times." Then Grandfather sat close and told me this story.

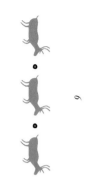

6

In the beginning, there was only the

●

land. Then the Great Being of the Sky placed

●

a woman, a man, and their sons on the earth.

●

Nothing else walked, swam, or flew.

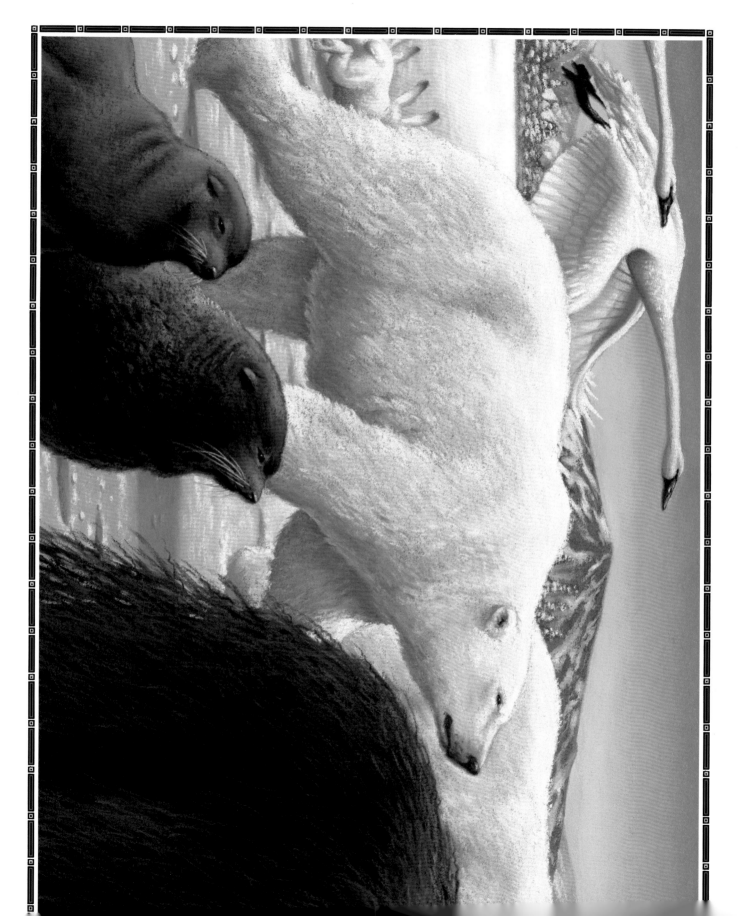

One day the Great Being of the Sky told the woman to dig a large hole in the ice. The woman walked until she came to the ice and then she started digging. She dug long and hard. When the hole was finished the woman stood back and waited. After awhile, an animal came out of the hole. Then another one, and another, and another.

As the last animal appeared from

the hole, the Great Being of the Sky told the

woman, "This is the caribou, the most important

gift of all, for the caribou will sustain you."

So the woman gave thanks and watched

the caribou run free. Over many seasons, the

caribou herd grew large and covered the land.

14

From the caribou the people received good meat to eat, warm clothes to wear, and dry tents of caribou hide.

But the sons hunted only the big and strong

●

caribou, leaving alone the small and sick. The sons

●

knew the weak ones had bad meat and poor skins.

In time, the weak and sick caribou out-

numbered the big and strong caribou. The sons

●

were upset and complained to the woman.

That night, the woman made magic to speak to the Great Being of the Sky. "There are too many weak and sick caribou," she said. "If we eat them, we will grow weak and sick also! Please give us a tool to cut the sickness from the caribou." The Great Being of the Sky listened to the woman and told her to go back to the hole in the ice, where she would find what was needed.

When the woman

reached the hole in the ice

she stared in amazement.

There stood a beautiful animal.

"This is Amorak, the Wolf,"

said the Great Being of the

Sky. "He and his children will

hunt the caribou and rid them

of the weak and the sick."

With great skill, the wolf and his children

● hunted the weaker caribou, leaving more land

● for the healthy. Soon the big and strong caribou

● covered the land once again, and the hunting was

● good for the wolf and for the sons of the woman.

"Now do you see why the wolf and the caribou are really brothers?" asked Grandfather. "Yes," I said. "The caribou feeds the wolf, but it is the wolf who keeps the caribou strong." Grandfather smiled and told me to sleep well.

28

Late that night, as I

lay warm beneath my blanket,

I heard again the long howl

of Amorak. I knew he was

calling his children to the hunt.

I closed my eyes and slept.

The tool had been found.

32